The Sw

by Bobby Lynn Maslen
pictures by John R. Maslen

Scholastic Inc.
New York Toronto London Auckland Sydney

Also available:

Bob Books
for Beginning Readers

Even More Bob Books
For Young Readers

For more Bob Books ask for them at your local bookstore or call: 1-800-733-5572.

ISBN 0-590-22453-0

Copyright © 1987 by Bobby Lynn Maslen.
All rights reserved. Published by Scholastic Inc., 555 Broadway, New York, NY 10012, by arrangement with Bob Books™ Publications.

12 11 10 9 8 7 6 5 4 3   5 6 7 8 9/9

Printed in the U.S.A.   10

First Scholastic printing, October 1994

It was summer. Pop, Stan, and Jim went to the pond.

Jim wanted to swim.
Stan wanted to swim.

Jim slipped into the pond.
Stan jumped into the pond.

Jim and Stan swam to a log.

"Step on the log, Jim", called Stan.
Jim slipped. "Jump on the log, Stan",
called Jim. Stan slid.

"Stop! Stop!" called Pop. The
log spun.

"Help, Pop", called Jim.
"Help us stop, Pop", called Stan.

Pop wanted to help Jim and Stan.
Pop jumped onto the log, but
the log was a trap.

Into the pond went Pop.
Pop got wet.

Pop, Stan, and Jim got out
of the pond.

"Sit in the sun, Jim. Sit in a warm spot, Stan", said Pop. "Sit in the warm sun, Pop," called Stan and Jim.

The three swimmers went to
a sunny spot. The wet swimmers
sat happily on a warm spot
in the sun.

The End

Book 4 adds:

Blends:

sw	-	swim
sp	-	spun
tr	-	trap
rm	-	warm

Long Vowel:

ee	-	three